Ryan's Dinosaur D

Written & Illustrated by Karl Dixon

Ryan doesn't just love dinosaurs, he lives, eats and dreams about dinosaurs!

He eats his dinner off dinosaur plates...

...and drinks his juice from a dinosaur cup...

...he dries off after a bath with his dinosaur towel...

...and gets into his dinosaur pyjamas...

...then Ryan's Dad comes upstairs to put him to bed and reads him a story from his dinosaur book...

...but when Ryan snuggles under his dinosaur duvet and goes to sleep...

...can you guess what he dreams about?

That's right, he dreams about dinosaurs.

He dreams of skiing with stegosaurus...

...or..

...trampolining with triceratops...

...or...

...teaching ballet to brontosaurus...

...or...

...trick or treating with tyrannosaurus-rex...

...or...

...tickling pterodactyl...

...or...

...running races with the raptors!

But when Ryan wakes up
from his dinosaur dreams...

...he quickly gets dressed
and rushes downstairs...

...to play with his dinosaurs all day until its his bed-time once more...

...and he can go to sleep and have more dinosaur dreams.

Printed in Great Britain
by Amazon.co.uk, Ltd.,
Marston Gate.